Revenge
of the Number Two

by

Bali Rai

First published in 2007 in Great Britain by
Barrington Stoke Ltd
18 Walker Street, Edinburgh, EH3 7LP

www.barringtonstoke.co.uk

Reprinted 2009

ISBN: 978-1-84299-474-0

Printed in Great Britain by Bell & Bain Ltd

A Note from the Author

One of the great things about writing a book for Barrington Stoke is that they never tell you what to write about. And this book proves that. How many other publishers would have let me write about a boy who poos in the swimming pool?

Revenge sort of follows on from another book I wrote for Barrington Stoke – *Two-Timer*. It's set in the same school and has some of the same characters and loads of new ones. And keen readers of *Two-Timer* will be happy to see that the goat is back.

I hope my next book will be set in the same school again. Maybe then the goat can get to be the star of the story at last!

Until then enjoy *Revenge* and try not to ever poo in the pool ...

Check out www.balirai.co.uk for more books.

Contents

Chapter 1
The Fart of Doom

Year Seven is always difficult. When you leave junior school, you can't wait to get to the big school. But then all the older kids tell you scare stories. You'll get your head flushed down the toilet. They'll push you off the bus. They'll glue you to the chairs in the dinner hall. And then you get to your new school and nothing really happens. OK, you get picked on by some of the older kids and the teachers are a bit scary, but mostly you just settle in and get on with things.

That's what I was doing in my Year Seven. I had some of my old friends, a load of new ones. I'd worked out where to go for my classes and how to keep away from the bullies. It was fine. *Until* we came back after Christmas. That's when my school life went down the toilet. And it was all because I hadn't gone. To the toilet ...

It was morning and my stomach felt well dodgy. It had felt bad since I woke up. Suddenly I really needed to go for a poo, but when I got to the boys' toilets there were three Year Eights outside the door. One of them, Mitesh, was nasty. Nasty to look at, nasty to smell. Just nasty. He saw me and said something to his mates. I froze to the spot. I tried to stop the "I need a dump right now" feeling. I gulped hard. My face started to go red. Mitesh grinned.

"What you got for me then, blood?" he asked. He was trying to sound like a bad boy.

I gave a shrug.

"Nuttin'," I told him. I went on clenching my bum cheeks together as hard as I could.

"You must have summat?" he said. In my head I saw him beating me up as the poo started to run down my legs.

But that didn't happen. Just as he was about to grab me, a Year Ten called Joey Beech ran past. He poked Mitesh in the eye with his finger. Mitesh began to howl like the fat, hairy gorilla that he was and I stepped back. Then him and his mates set off after Joey.

I felt great now. It was like I was lying in the warm sea on a beach. I stepped towards the door of the toilets. Nearly there ... and then the buzzer went for lessons. The corridor was suddenly full of pupils and teachers. One minute I was all alone, about to open the door, and the next a wave of kids was sweeping me along the corridor, on to somewhere else. My arse cheeks were still clenched tight. In the crowd were two girls from my class, Lexie and Beckie. They began to talk to me about lipstick and if Lexie should kiss Sam Goldberg in Year Nine. I told them Lexie could kiss Sam if she wanted – what did it have to do with me? By then we were in our form room, and it was register time.

"Kully Singh?" called out Mr Grant who was our form tutor.

"Yessir ..." I said. By now even talking was hard.

In my belly I could feel gases bubble. They were going round and round like socks in a washing machine. I needed to fart. Badly. I tried to hold it in, all that gas, but it started to make its way out. Suddenly I couldn't hold it any more and I farted. It was a slow-go job – silent but deadly. It smelled like something dead too, something that had been dead for a thousand years. Like them Egyptian mummies and that.

"EUUURGHHH!!!!!!!!" shouted Lexie and Beckie together.

"BLEEEEEUGHHHHHHHHHHHHH!!!!!!!!!!!" screeched Ben, one of my new friends.

"JEEZ!!!!!" shouted Mr Grant. "What the hell is that – a stink-bomb?"

For a minute I sat still. I thought I wouldn't say anything. Then – I don't know what for – I turned to my left. Ragandesh Sivaratnam was sitting there. He never said or did anything. I got it in my head to blame him.

"EHHHHHHHHHHHHHHHHHH!!!!!!!!!!!!!!! Ragandesh!!!!" I shouted out.

One by one the other kids turned to him and started to laugh. Ragandesh just sat there and took it, like he always did. He seemed to shrink back into the chair. He looked smaller and smaller. But his eyes were burning and he was looking at me. There was hurt there. Pain maybe. He looked like he didn't believe what I'd done. I felt about the same size as my dad's feet – that's really small. I turned away. But farting had helped. I felt a whole lot better.

"Right, 7G! Stop laughing at that poor lad and get to the PE department ... and Ragandesh ... er ... come and see me, please," said Mr Grant.

I grabbed my bag and went on ahead with Ben and a lad called Danny.

"That was so nasty," Danny laughed.

"Smelt like your mum's breath," Ben said.

"Like yer dad's armpits more like," added Danny.

I just laughed along. I was glad that it wasn't me they were poking fun at. Not about the fart, anyway.

PE lesson that day was swimming and we walked with two more classes round to the local swimming pool on Downing Drive. The walk only took a few minutes but I started to feel bad again. A dull pain started to throb in my belly. I could feel more gases begin to build up. I needed to fart but I was stuck between Lexie and Beckie again. This time they were linking arms with me and singing really badly. I tried to get away from them but they just held on. All I could think about was not pooing in my pants.

By the time I was in the pool I was hanging on for dear life. Not to the side of the pool. To *my* insides. I was gonna have to go any minute. How embarrassing would it be to get out of the pool and ask Miss Hammerhead if I could go to the toilet. And then, what if the toilets stank after I'd finished? Everyone would know it was me. They'd have seen me getting out of the pool to go to the toilet. What was I going to do?

Ben and Danny splashed past me and pulled me with them. And then the last fart of all started. The Fart of Doom.

It was slow and sure. I knew I had to dive for the bottom of the pool so no one would see the bubbles come out of the water round me. My head was yelling "*DIVE! DIVE!*" like Chelsea's manager to one of his players. I dived down to the bottom of the pool. I knew down there my fart'd make a few bubbles but it wouldn't smell as bad and I'd be away from everyone. I relaxed a bit as the fart worked its way out.

But that was the problem. I relaxed a bit too much. Something floated past me and headed up to the top of the water. As I swam up I saw all the other kids getting out of the

water. They were shouting and pointing.
I looked around. Who could I blame? There
was no one. By the time I'd swum to the
edge, everyone was out of the pool except me.
And they all stood there laughing and
pointing. Even Danny was grinning. *And* the
teachers. Only Ben, Lexie and Beckie weren't
laughing. They just looked embarrassed. I
shoved my head under the water to drown
out the shouts. And so no one would see
me cry ...

Chapter 2
Mr Number Two

After that things just got worse. The rest of Year Seven was just a blur. People shouting at me in the corridor, calling me silly names. Crap Pants, Shitty Shoes, Poo Head – all sorts of stuff. Even one of the teachers had a go – a young English teacher called Mr Simms. He's one of those teachers who likes to think he's down with the kids and that. Talks about the latest bands and uses gangster slang. He's a total knob. And he's the one who called me Number Two for the first time.

It was at lunchtime at the start of Year Eight. After the summer holidays. I was hoping that everyone had forgotten about my accident in the pool. Fat chance of that. There's this crew – the 2.2 Massive – who pick on me all the time. That Mitesh is one of them. They're only in the year above me at school but they act like they're big men. They stand around in the corridors and get at the young kids. They think they're rappers. Anyway I was walking past two of them, Dipesh and Suresh, when Dipesh smacked me on the back of my head. I turned round and swore at him and then ran. Ben was with me. He saw Mr Simms nearby and went over to tell him what had happened. Then Mr Simms set off after us.

By the time Dipesh got near me I was in the music room. I was trying to hide behind a set of drums. Dipesh walked into the music room with a big grin on his face.

"Can't hide from me, Shitpants ..." he shouted.

I looked around. Where could I go? There was no escape – the only exit was the windows and they were locked. Maybe I could run past Dipesh but he was really fat and he was blocking the door. In the end I just stood up. I knew I was going to get a beating. When I stood, Dipesh grinned like a shark.

"OK, Shitpants ... left any more tings in da pool?"

I looked at him and began to get angry. I tried not to say anything but it was no good.

"Yeah – yer mum," I told him.

His eyes screwed up and he looked like he was going to explode.

"You're dead, you little – !" he began.

"*LEAVE IT!*" I heard a teacher shout from the door.

I began to grin. I was safe, for now.

"But he just had a go at me mum, innit ..." Dipesh said.

Mr Simms held up his hands.

"Listen, blood," he said to Dipesh. "Jus' lef' it ... it ain't worth the grief, you get me?"

I looked at Mr Simms. I held back a smirk. The man was a fool. What did he think he sounded like!?

"Jus' get out of here, blood," he said to Dipesh.

"Ain't no blood o' yours," muttered Dipesh. Then he looked right at me. "And you ain't outta da woods or nuttin' yet, Poobreath."

He turned and walked out of the door as Mr Simms came over to me and switched back to his real voice.

"Who do we have here?" he asked.

"Kully Singh – 8G," I told him.

Something moved across his face, like a shadow. The corners of his mouth turned up. He started to walk out of the room.

"Come, on," he said to me.

As we walked into the corridor, Ben was waiting for me with Lexie and Beckie. There were also loads of other kids there. Mr Simms turned to me and grinned.

"If I was you, Mr Number Two," he said, "I'd stay away from those lads."

He walked off. I could tell he was feeling all clever and smug. The other pupils ran off laughing. Lexie tried to hold onto me as I went mad.

"It's OK, Kully – he's just a dickhead," she said to me as she grabbed my arm.

"*Nah* – you got ripped by the stupidest teacher in the whole school!" shouted a lad called Marcus.

Three or four other kids joined in and I felt the tears starting. I turned left into the PE corridor and ran. I didn't stop running until I was at the school gates, where I paused for a moment to wipe away the tears. Then I ran all the way home.

****

When I got back to school the next day I had to go and see my head of year. He's a science teacher called Mr Brimstone. I sat outside his office as other pupils walked past. They were all sniggering and whispering. I was fed up. I just wanted to leave, go to another school. If I didn't I was going to get teased for the rest of my life.

Then I heard Mr Brimstone.

"*BOY!*" he shouted.

I jumped up out of the chair.

"Sir?"

"Absence from school? And no note? In you come, son," he added, much more softly.

His office was enormous. It had wooden panels on the walls and there was the faint smell of cigarettes and farms. I looked at him.

"Sir?" I began.

"What?" he asked.

"Why does it smell of – ?" I started to say.

"Ah," he cut in, "that'll be the goat."

As if by magic a big grey goat poked its head round his desk and bleated at me. I looked at it and forgot all about being in trouble. All I could think about was why my head of year had a goat in his office. Mr Brimstone knew that's what I was thinking.

"My wife won't let me keep the goat at home and it's an interesting science project," he went on. The goat bleated again and then swung its head from side to side.

But I just got more puzzled.

"Is he like a pet or summat?" I asked.

"Be quiet. Now tell me why you think you can walk out of school whenever you like. And leave nothing out. And I don't want any more questions about the bloody goat," he insisted.

I thought about telling him the truth but I wasn't that stupid. Like he'd believe that I was being picked on by kids *and* teachers. I told him that I wasn't feeling well.

"My uncle died," I lied, and then I felt bad about it right away. But then again I did have about 50 uncles. What did it matter?

"I'm very sorry to hear that," he said. "But you still don't have the right to walk out. A note from your parents, boy. For tomorrow, please."

"But ..." I began. Where was I gonna get a note from? Maybe I'd get Lexie and Beckie to write me one.

"No buts. Now, off you toddle," added Mr Brimstone.

"Sir," I muttered.

As I turned to walk out, the goat looked at me. I swear it was laughing at me. In my head I heard something bleating, "*Shitty pants, shitty pants ...*" I shook my head and went to my maths lesson.

****

After school I walked to the bus stop with Beckie and Lexie. We were talking about girl stuff. Well, they were talking and I was being moody. The bus stop is in a village called Dinton and the girls were walking so slowly that it took fifteen minutes to get there instead of five.

"I'm going to get some chocolate," I told them. "You two want anything?"

"A handsome prince!" they both said at the same time. I swear they were twins.

I shook my head and walked into the newsagents. There was a whole load of Year Sevens I had to push past. The shop had four rows of shelves and I picked the third row – that's where the chocolate was. As I stood and tried to work out which chocolate I was going to eat, someone came up behind me and pulled on my ear.

"OWW!" I shouted and span round. It was Jitinder and Mitesh both from the 2.2 Massive. Like I said, they're in the year above me and they think they're so special.

"You think you can make a monkey out of me, blood?" asked Mitesh with a sneer.

"No ... no ... I ..." I started to say.

Mitesh grabbed my nose with his thumb and finger and started to twist it. It hurt like hell. Tears started in my eyes and I couldn't breathe. I shoved at him but he was so lardy that my hands just sank into his belly. He carried on for what felt like ages and then he stopped.

"Next time it'll be a whole lot worser, you get me?" he warned.

That's when I felt something being rubbed into the back of my head. It was a chocolate bar.

"Now you can be a real shithead, innit!" Jitinder yapped, as he pushed the chocolate into my hair.

"EUUURH!!!!" I shouted. I tried to get away then Mitesh stuck out his leg and I tripped over it and fell on the floor.

"What's the matter?" another kid asked. "Done it in yer pants again?"

The other kids in the shop started laughing. I felt like my whole world was on action replay. I jumped up and ran out of the shop. I began to try and get the chocolate out of my hair. It was all soft so it stuck to my head and hands. I ran past Beckie and Lexie and they tried to stop me. I ran off, away from them and into a little park. As I got to the swings it started to rain. The chocolate and the rain all mixed together and began to run down my face and neck, onto my clothes. I stood and let it happen. All I wanted was to zap myself away to another world.

Chapter 3
The 2.2 Massive

Year Nine was better. Less people called me "Number Two" and I even made some more friends. The kids in my form group started talking to me. Before, they'd just whispered about me or laughed when I walked into the room. Now they were chatting and being nice. It was great. Some of them even gave me cards on my birthday. Everything started to work out. And Lexie started telling me how much she liked me too.

"You're lovely, Kully," she said to me, one break time, as we were walking out of maths.

"So are you," I told her. "You're really funny."

I didn't have a clue that what she really meant was she fancied me. Even when she carried on telling me, it still didn't click.

"But you're *really* lovely," she said again.

"Er ... thanks," I muttered.

"*Really, really* lovely," she added.

"Er ... OK. I ... er ..." I said, like a fool.

I didn't know what else to say because I didn't understand what she was getting at.

"Oh, never mind!" said Lexie in a huff.

Then Lexie and Beckie walked off hand in hand. I was left standing where I was. Random things went round and round in my head. Like how do they put the jam in doughnuts? And why did I feel like I'd said or done something wrong? By the time my duh-brain had started to work properly again, it was time for English.

Down at the end of the corridor I saw the door to Mr Brimstone's office was open. At least I thought it was. And I swear it was the goat that had opened it. Now the goat was giving me the evil eye, looking hard at me. But when I shook my head, the goat had gone.

"You OK?" Ben asked.

"Er ... yeah ..." I told him.

****

Not everything that happened in Year Nine was good. And that was because of the 2.2 Massive. They made my life hell. It started in the history area just before Christmas.

I was sitting on a radiator with Ben and we were talking about football. I heard some people shouting and turned to see my cousin, Harj, who was in the same year as me. He never really talked to me at school. Not after the swimming pool thing. He'd said he'd felt bad for me about that, and sorry for laughing, but I still didn't like him much.

That day, Harj was having an argument with Jitinder from the 2.2 Massive. I hated Jitinder so I felt like backing up my cousin, even if he was a git. I got off the radiator and stepped closer. Jitinder was calling Harj names.

"You start a fight, if you is so bad," he said, in his squeaky voice.

"Get yer mum to start it," Harj said back. "Oh, no – she can't, can she? She's so fat she can't get on a bus. She has to wait for a crane to lift her up and drop her at the shops."

"Get lost!" shouted Jitinder. "I'm gonna mash you up if you say anyt'ing else 'bout my mum."

But Harj just went on. "And I heard that she was so big they made her into a continent last week. She fills half the map of the world ..."

"You ...!"

Jitinder swore and tried to hit Harj. Harj just stepped to one side and Jitinder crashed down onto the tables and chairs. Harj looked at me, winked and then walked off.

Jitinder was just lying on the floor. His bag strap was round his head and his hair was all over the place. Like an idiot I started to laugh. Jitinder looked at me but he didn't do anything.

I thought that I'd got away with it. But I was wrong. Laughing at him was a big mistake.

The next day things began to go wrong. I was sitting on the same radiator. This time Lexie and Beckie were banging on to me about something, when Mitesh, Jitinder and the rest of the 2.2 Massive walked past. I didn't look at them. I thought they'd leave me alone, but I was wrong. Mitesh grabbed my bag, then he ran over to the window, opened it, and threw my bag out.

"Oi!" I shouted, and jumped up. "My iPod's in there!"

"It was," laughed Mitesh. "Now it's all over the ground. Out there."

Jitinder gave me a dirty look.

"That'll teach you to laugh at me, you shithead ..." he said softly.

"Later's, Number Two," added Mitesh. The two of them walked off.

The history area's on the second floor of our school building. The ground's a long way down. I walked over to the window and looked out. My bag was lying in a puddle and all my things were all over the place. I could see my lovely new iPod half in the puddle. I felt sick. I ran downstairs and out of the building. The girls ran down too. My iPod was broken, and some of my other stuff too. The fountain pen in my bag had broken and there was ink on everything. I swore. Beckie and Lexie helped me pick up my things.

"My dad's gonna kill me," I told them.

"No, he won't," Beckie said. "Just tell him what happened. He'll understand."

But that was just it. How would he understand? I'd never told him anything. He didn't know about the bullying, the teasing. Most of all, he didn't know about what had happened in the swimming pool. How could I tell him? He'd never look at me in the same way again.

I was so mad about my bag that the next day I walked right up to Mitesh and hit him. He looked at me in shock. Like me punching him was the last thing he expected. And then he started to laugh.

"You call that a punch, you dickhead?" he growled. "My baby sister hits harder than that."

I didn't know what to say. I stood there and looked at him, just like he'd been looking at me. And then he punched me back. It hurt. I fell backwards onto the floor and I started to cry.

"Yeah – you do that, you poof!" Mitesh sneered. "Always gonna be just a Number Two ..."

I didn't tell my dad how I'd got punched or about the iPod. My dad grounded me for two weeks because of the mess my bag was in and all the stuff that had got broken. I got into trouble at school too.

My life was a mess. I was a joke. I hadn't even hit Mitesh right. I felt useless. No matter how much my friends tried to make me feel OK, it didn't work. I felt like I was a waste of space.

Chapter 4
Personal Trainer

It was in the summer between Years Nine and Ten that something in me changed. I'd had enough of being called names. I didn't want to feel weak any more. I wanted to do something to change my life. And the reason for the change was my grandfather.

Gramps came to stay with us that summer holiday. My Gramps was big and strong. His arms were massive, and every morning he got up early and went for a five-mile run. After he'd been at our house a week he woke me up one morning at six a.m.

"Gerrup!" he shouted.

"Huh?" I groaned from under my duvet.

"Come on, boy. Look lively!" Gramps said.

"Gramps ...!" I moaned.

"Gerr outta bed," he went on. "I haven't seen you much since I got here. What are you – a ghost? Always flopping on the sofa like the world owes you a living."

"But ..." I began.

But Gramps wasn't having any of it. He came over to my bed and pulled the duvet off me. I didn't even stop him. I felt too weak.

"We're going on a run," he told me. "Now go and get your gym shoes."

"You mean trainers?" I asked. I was beginning to wake up now.

"Yes – now hurry up. You're making me late ..." Gramps said.

"Late for what?" I wanted to know. "The sunrise?"

"The sun's already up, boy," he told me. "Birds in the trees singing ... let's go, my duck!"

I need to tell you something about my Gramps. He spent a long time in the army. That's why he gets up early. And it's why he's still so fit and active, even when he's 75. He's always going for runs and doing weights and stuff. He's amazing.

We ran for about four miles. Then my legs began to feel like jelly. I sat down on the ground. I felt sick. I wanted to throw up. Gramps stopped, walked back and stood over me.

"I was just like you once," he told me. "Weak and wimpy. I worked hard to become what I am now."

"Gramps ...!" I moaned.

"Shurrup and listen, boy," he insisted.

"What?" I asked.

"There's something wrong with you. I can see it in the way you walk. The way you talk. It's in your eyes ..." Gramps began.

What he was on about? I asked myself. And then I got this creeping feeling that he knew. Everything. He didn't, of course. What he *did* know was that I was feeling down. Even if he didn't know why.

"So," he went on. "You can tell me why you walk around with a face like a backside that's been slapped. Or you can run for another four miles ... until you really do throw up."

"But – "

Gramps shook his head.

"No buts," he told me. "Now gerrup and walk back to the house. You can tell me on the way."

I began to tell him other stuff. I didn't tell him the truth. But he knew I was hiding something and in the end I just told him. Everything. All about the swimming pool thing and the names and the bullying. He listened to what I was saying. He didn't say a word. When I was done, we were near home and he stopped me in the street.

"*They* don't need to know any of this," he told me. He meant my parents.

"Thanks," I said.

"Don't thank me," he went on. "I'm here for all of your holiday. Every day we're going to get up at five o'clock and run. Then I'm going to show you how to lift weights. By the time I'm done with you, those bullies will be running scared."

"But I can't be like you," I moaned. "I'm not the same as you. You're big and strong. I'm just a boy ..."

"No, Kully," he insisted and he looked right at me. "You aren't a boy any more. You're a man. Start acting like it."

****

Later that day Gramps went to the shops. He came back with a big box. He set it down in the hallway and told me to get him some water.

"That was heavy," he said.

"What is it?" I asked.

"Weights," he grinned. "Now go and get your sports kit on and let's get going ..."

I got changed and Gramps took me into the garage where my dad had a weights bench and one set of weights. He opened the box and started to get the new ones out. He told me to start doing some stretches.

"Stretch out those arms and legs," he said. "Get the blood flowing, my duck."

Then he got me to lie on the weights bench. Above me was a long bar with a heavy iron disc at each end.

"Take some deep breaths," Gramps said, "and then put your hands here and here on that bar."

He took my hands and put them in the right place. The bar felt cold and my hands were damp with sweat. The iron discs on the bar looked really heavy.

"I'm not sure I can lift them," I said.

"Just shurrup and work at it," Gramps told me. "Focus on the bar ..."

I did as he said. Then suddenly, Gramps lifted the bar up. He didn't warn me and my hands and arms lifted up along with the bar.

"OWWWW!!!!!!!" I groaned, as I had to bring the weights and the bar down.

"Are you a baby?" Gramps shouted. "Stop crying! I'm going to bring the bar down to rest and then I want you to push it up again. Just one rep ..."

"What's a rep?" I asked.

"Each time you lift the bar and bring it down – that's one rep," Gramps told me.

"Oh," I said softly.

"And to begin with," he went on, "you'll do five reps for each set and you'll do three sets."

"Huh?" I said. I didn't understand.

"A set is when you do some reps in a row," Gramps went on. "Are you *that* stupid? Now *lift*!" he shouted. He helped me to push the bar up again, but this time I had to do more of the lifting.

Pain shot down my arms and across my back. It was torture. Then, as soon as I had got the bar lifted, I had to bring it slowly back down again.

"There," said Gramps with a grin. "Not perfect but OK. Now do it again. On your own this time ..."

By the time I'd done my three sets I was worn out. I never knew that lifting weights took so much out of you. My arms and back were burning. Not that Gramps was bothered.

"Right!" he ordered. "Get on that gym mat – I want 20 stomach crunches."

That first time in the garage was murder. When Gramps let me go at last I couldn't feel a thing. Not in my arms, legs, stomach. Not anywhere. He was a real bully. But I still did it again the next day, and the day after that and every day, except Sundays, for the rest of the school holiday.

And then one day, about a week before school started again, I looked at myself in the mirror. I had muscles. Muscles! And my stomach was harder and flatter than I'd ever seen it. Some of my clothes had even started to get tight around the tops of my arms. I felt great! I went out in a T-shirt. I looked at the other kids with their skinny arms and baggy jeans and I felt really proud. Like a superhero.

****

Two days later Gramps had to go home.

"Those bullies ... are you gonna run scared of them now?" he asked.

"Nah ... I reckon when they next see me they'll be doin' the running! And it'll all be down to you, Gramps," I said.

"Remember this, son. Revenge is a dish best served cold ..."

I looked at him. Had he been drinking? What was he on about?

"What does that mean?" I asked.

"Bloody schools today!" he moaned. "Don't they teach you anything but tyin' your shoelaces?"

"Er ..." I muttered.

"I'm not saying you need to get back at those bullies and get revenge," Gramps said. "But if you *are* going to, make sure you plan it all the way – like it's a battle."

"But I wasn't going to take revenge," I insisted.

"No?" Gramps went on. "So there'll be no Revenge of the Number Two, then?"

When Gramps said my nickname out loud – the name I hated – I began to remember all the rubbish I'd had at school. But then Gramps winked at me. I knew what he was doing. He was showing me words don't matter. They're just words.

"Now make us a cup of soddin' tea," he shouted. "I'm bleedin' parched, my duck ..."

Chapter 5
New Start?

On my first day back at school I got some weird looks. A girl called Mina Patel walked up to me at lunchtime and told me I looked buff.

"What's that mean?" I asked. She didn't tell me. Instead she went back over to her friends, who were all giggling.

"I think she likes you," said Ben, who was in front of me in the lunch queue.

I heard someone shout, "Get lost, Harj!" My cousin Harj was talking to his best mate, Marcus. Marcus was asking him about some girl called Kelly. I looked over at him, then I turned back to Ben.

"You seen the girls?" I asked him.

Ben nodded towards the back of the dinner hall.

"Over there. Beckie's got a new haircut ..." he hissed.

I looked over to where the girls were sitting. When I saw Lexie, something in my head went pop. She looked different. I got my food and Ben and I went to sit down. We found a table just next to where the girls were sitting.

"Hey, Lexie!" I said.

"Kully!" she said with a big smile. "You look great!"

I went a bit red but inside I felt dead good.

Lexie blushed and looked away. I wanted to say something else but I didn't know what. In the end I just turned to Ben and started banging on about the new football season.

****

For the first few weeks people were mostly different with me. Most of the lads in my year stopped calling me names and I had loads more friends. I got asked out about ten times too, but that was by girls who I didn't fancy. So I kept saying I wasn't interested.

I felt great. I was happier than before and popular too. That's the best way in our school. People started to invite me to parties and the really cool people started to say hello to me.

But it wasn't all change. I still had the 2.2 Massive on my case. They got me in my second week back. As I walked into the art and science block I bumped right into the 2.2 Massive. All six of them.

"Check out Number Two, blood!" laughed Mitesh.

"You been takin' steroids, you knob?" asked Jitinder.

The rest of them started laughing at me and for a moment I got scared. But then I remembered what my Gramps had said about never letting bullies get to you. I stopped still and looked right at Mitesh.

"Yes, battyhole!" I said to him. "You been in the ugly clinic again? Tried to get a facelift or something?"

"You what?" he said, all aggressive.

"You heard me," I said. I stayed where I was and went on looking at him.

"Nah!" said one of the other lads. His name was Matt Peavey and he was a skinny Eminem fan. He looked over at Mitesh. "How you gonna let him blaps you down, blood!" he said.

I was just turning to Matt to ask him what the hell he was talking about. Jitinder and Mitesh both jumped me. The rest of them joined in. When they were done, I was lying on the floor, bleeding out of my nose and mouth and every bit of my body hurt.

"You better watch it, Number Two," warned Mitesh, as he walked away. "Nex' time gon' be worse, innit ..."

I groaned. I started thinking about Gramps. He'd never told me how to deal with six lads all at the same time.

Two hours later I was in Mr Brimstone's office. I was cleaned up, with plasters all over my face.

"You fell down the *stairs?*" Mr Brimstone asked for the fifth time.

"Yessir," I said. My nose throbbed with pain.

"And you expect me to believe that?" Mr Brimstone went on.

"Yessir," I said again.

Mr Brimstone lit his pipe. He drew in a load of nasty thick smoke.

"I thought you weren't supposed to smoke in school no more?" I said. I knew I was pushing my luck.

"Would you like another trip down the stairs, Singh?" asked Mr Brimstone.

"Er ... no, sir," I said.

"Right, well, shut up then and bugger off!" Mr Brimstone growled.

I turned and walked out of his room. As I went left, towards the science labs, I saw the goat. It was walking slowly towards me, looking at me all the time. Its horns looked a lot bigger than before. They looked scary too – all sharp and that. As it got near me, it stopped and turned its head all the way round, like it was the devil. And then it bleated at me. I swear it said, "*Revenge, revenge ...* " but I didn't stop to find out. I shook my head and walked away. In fact, I *limped* away ...

Chapter 6
The Fittest Girl in School

Every year, just before we break up for Christmas, the school puts on a show. It's called the Christmas Special. Pupils from every year practise for months to star in it. They do a bit of drama or some poetry. The lower years get to wear fancy dress. Some of them even sing and dance. And it always ends with a blockbuster Grand Finale. A big finish. The school band plays a big hit or something. I have to say, I'd never been to the Christmas Special. In fact I never really thought about it until one Saturday in November, halfway through that first term of Year Ten.

Me and Lexie had been getting really close and at last I'd worked out that she fancied me. That was only after Beckie had told me. Loud and clear.

"You're a fool," Beckie told me. She'd rung me for a chat that Saturday. I was at home, watching telly and eating my breakfast.

"Why?" I wanted to know.

"Did Lexie ask you to go round to hers today?" Beckie said.

Lexie *had* asked me. Two days before. She'd said something about going round to hers to watch a DVD and work on a science project together. But I'm a big Liverpool fan and they were playing live. I'd told her that I was going to be busy.

"Yeah," I told Beckie. "Lexie did say something like that."

"See what I mean?" Beckie told me. "She *fancies* you, you idiot."

"What?" I didn't know what else to say. I just sat where I was, a big smile on my face. Because I fancied her too.

"She's the fittest girl in school and she wants to go out with you ..." Beckie said. "Get your arse over there!"

"But Liverpool are playing," I moaned.

"Do you want me to come round and drag you to Lexie's by your pubes?" Beckie went on.

I didn't even need to think about it. I believed that Beckie would do what she'd said. She was mad.

"OK," I said. "What time shall I go, then?"

"About three o'clock," Beckie told me. "And go to Asda on the way. Take her some flowers."

"Why?" I asked.

"Stop being such an idiot and just do what I say, d'you understand?" Beckie said before she hung up. She sounded like a teacher. Or my mum.

"OK, then," I said.

I put the phone down and went to put my cornflakes bowl in the kitchen. My parents had gone out and the sink was full of washing up. I thought about doing it but I didn't bother. Instead I stood and stared out of the kitchen window. I was thinking about Lexie.

When I got to Lexie's house she let me in with a big smile. She took me into the living room. She looked great. Her brown hair was longer than before and she was wearing a white dress with thin shoulder straps. It had big red flowers printed on it. She had jeans on and pink Converse trainers. She smelt amazing – like strawberries. I couldn't stop looking at her.

"You can sit down," she said. I was just standing there, holding the flowers I'd got for her.

I started looking at her chest. Then I stopped and blushed. She smiled at me.

"Are those flowers for me?" she asked.

"Er ... yeah. I thought you'd like them ..." I muttered.

She pushed her hair away from her face and one of the dress straps fell down. I watched. Lexie grinned and pulled it back up.

"You mean Beckie told you it would be a good idea?" she said, before laughing at me.

"Did she tell you?" I asked. I felt all embarrassed.

"'Course she did," Lexie said. "She rang me right after she'd spoken to you."

"So is what Beckie said right?" I asked. Lexie walked towards me and took the flowers.

Something in my belly started to whirl round and round, and a warm feeling started working its way up my legs.

"About what?" Lexie said with a smile.

Her face was so close now that I could almost feel her lips about to touch mine. I felt myself move back, just a little. But then Lexie kissed me.

"Yes," she said, when she'd pulled back.

I didn't say anything. I couldn't do anything. My hands and feet and something else were tingling. I couldn't even move. Well, er ...

Lexie grinned at me.

"You're fit, Kully," she told me. She threw the flowers on the sofa and then kissed me again. In my head something went *Bang!*

Later on, after we'd snogged for ages, we were lying on her sofa. We weren't watching the DVD she'd put on. Instead we were just talking about stuff. All kinds of stuff. It was Lexie who started talking about the 2.2 Massive.

"They're doing a rap for the Christmas Special," she told me.

"But they're rubbish," I said. "They can't rap to save their lives! Remember when they did that thing in assembly during Year Eight?"

Lexie giggled.

"Yeah," she said. "The lights didn't work and Jitinder sounded like he was a girl, his voice was so high!"

"And that rap ... how'd it go again?" I added.

"Yo, yo! Yo! Yo! Yo!" Lexie started to laugh. "That was all it was ..."

"Yeah, and Matt Peavey was doing that human beat-box thing. He sounded like he was farting outta his mouth!"

"And when Mr Brimstone took them off stage, they were acting as if they had play guns and all!" Lexie went on.

"Yeah, yeah!" I said. "That was *so* funny ..."

Lexie smiled.

"So how come they're getting to do the show this year?" I asked. "Everyone knows they're crap."

"I dunno, but they're not just doing the show. They're gonna end it. They're doing the Grand Finale."

I shook my head.

"The Grand Finale – how did they swing that?" I asked.

"I dunno," she told me. "I asked Mr Simms and he started talking like a rudeboy."

I nodded.

"Yeah – why *does* he do that?" I wanted to know.

"Dunno," said Lexie. "But we've got a plan, me and Ben and Beckie. We're gonna get back at the 2.2 Massive. We're going to make them sorry. At the Christmas Special."

"How?" I asked.

"Never mind that," she said. "You talk too much. Don't you want to kiss me?"

I did.

****

On Monday I was walking out of history when I saw my cousin Harj. He told me he was helping with the plan too.

"Easy, Kully! I hear you're going to get the 2.2 Massive back?" he said.

"How'd you know 'bout that?" I asked.

"Your mates asked me to help," Harj said. "They asked Marcus too."

"What you got against them?" I wanted to know.

"Ain't you heard?" he asked.

I didn't know anything about Harj and the 2.2 Massive.

"I was seeing Mitesh's sister," Harj said.

"What, Neeta?" I couldn't believe it.

I was shocked. Harj was known around school as a virgin. He'd never even kissed a girl.

"Yeah ... and I was seein' this other girl too," he added.

"Get lost!" I shouted.

"Serious. Anyway, I got caught out and Mitesh gave me a load of grief," he went on.

"But Neeta's goin' out with Jag," I said. "I see them all the time, fighting and that."

He nodded. "She is now. I'm with the other girl."

"Who?" I asked.

"She don't go to this school," he told me. "She's called Kelly."

I nodded.

"So you wanna get back at Mitesh, then?" I asked him.

"Yeah – and Jitinder too," said Harj.

I asked Harj what he knew about the plan. But he just grinned and shook his head.

"I ain't allowed to tell you," he said. "But don't worry. When the shit goes down, you'll be there ..."

He must have seen something in my face twitch when he said "shit".

"Oh, yeah," he grinned. "Sorry, mate."

I told him it was OK and walked off to the loo. When I got there, Mr Brimstone's goat was drinking a bowl of water outside the toilets. I turned round before it saw me. I went to the toilets in the next block.

Chapter 7
Go with the Flow

I'm not going to tell you about everything that went on before the night of the school show. All I'll say is that there was *something*. The next day, a gang of builders turned up to work on the school theatre. Someone said there was a problem with the stage. The headteacher – her name's Mrs Pincher – was running around like a mad woman.

"We *must* get that stage fixed. It'll be a disaster – a disaster!" she said as she passed me and Beckie in the main corridor.

"What's up with her?" I asked Beckie.

"There's a problem with the stage," said Beckie. "They're having to use the sports hall to practise for the show."

I gave a shrug.

"Great," I said.

"Yeah!" said Beckie. "I gave Mrs Pincher my dad's number ..."

Beckie's dad was a builder.

"Is he doing the job?" I asked, not thinking anything of it.

"Yeah," Beckie said. "He's there right now."

****

At the end of the day, I saw a load of vans parked up by the theatre. Beckie was talking to a short man with a skinhead haircut and tattoos all over his massive arms. It was her dad. I walked across to say hello to them. I was waiting for Lexie.

"Hello, Kully," said Beckie's dad.

"Hello, Mr Clapper."

"Call me Dave," he said with a grin.

"What's up with the stage?" I asked. I saw some of workmen carrying bags of cement into the theatre. They were really big bags, too.

"Dodgy work," he told me. "Some plonker ain't bedded the stage in properly. Used two and three mix instead of ..."

He went on talking but I'd stopped listening. I started thinking about food. I was starving. Anyway I didn't have a clue what he was talking about. When I saw him stop talking, I said, "Oh, really?"

"How long will the work take, Dad?" asked Beckie.

"Could be *hours*," he told her. "Long enough for me to get you that laptop you want for Christmas."

He winked at her and Beckie grinned.

When Lexie got there, she saw the builders by the theatre. She looked at Beckie, and asked what was happening. Lexie and Beckie looked at each other in a funny way but I didn't think about it. I was too busy looking at Lexie's chest.

"The stage is falling down," Beckie told Lexie. "My dad's sorting it out."

"Let's go and look," said Lexie.

They both skipped off. I went after them. When I got to the vans, the workmen were rolling big blue plastic containers out of a truck. There were ten of them. They were all blue with black lids. Next to them were three long bits of metal.

"You wanna watch that," one of the workmen said to the other one. He was talking about one of the blue containers.

"Why's that, then?" his mate asked.

"Never you mind," said the first. "Jus' gerron wiv it ..."

****

I had my tea at Lexie's house. I called my mum to check if that was OK. After tea, Beckie and Ben came over. All four of us sat in Lexie's room. We listened to music and looked at stupid stuff on the internet. Ben showed me a website called *YoMama.com* which made us both laugh. It was a website all about jokes to do with mums.

"Here's another good joke," I said. "Yo mama so fat, when she steps on a scale it reads 'to be continued ...'"

"That's horrible!" Beckie said, but she couldn't stop grinning.

"This one's my favourite," Ben told her. "Yo mama so stupid, her idea of safe sex is locking the car doors!"

At that one we all burst out laughing. When all the laughing had cooled down, I asked them about the show.

"So are you going to tell me what's going on tomorrow?" I wanted to know.

"Nope!" said Beckie. "All you need to know is the signal."

"What signal?" I asked. I didn't understand what they were on about. They hadn't told me about a signal.

Beckie winked at me and then made a face. It looked like someone was cleaning out her stomach with a hoover or she was about to throw up. She turned to me. "When I make that face, you have to come out from where you're hiding and do what I tell you …"

"Where am I hiding?" I asked. I was getting stressed now. I definitely did not understand.

"Just go with the flow, innit?" she said as if she was one of the 2.2 Massive.

At that second Ben started giggling.

"What you found now?" asked Lexie.

"It's another joke," he said. "It's brilliant. Yo mama so ugly, when she joined the ugly contest they said 'sorry, no professionals'!"

The rest of them started laughing again. I just sat where I was. *What were they going to do at the Christmas Special?* I asked myself. I had butterflies in my stomach just thinking about it.

Chapter 8
Rudeboy

The next school day went really quickly. It was the end of term so we didn't do much in the lessons. After lunch, the pupils who were in the show went off to have their last practice. My last lesson was maths. There were only about ten of us in class so the teacher let us just sit around and chat.

"Where's Lexie?" I asked Beckie.

Beckie winked again.

"She's down at the practice," she said.

"But she ain't performing in the show," I said.

"That's what you think, you silly little boy," she giggled.

"Beckie, please ..." I tried to ask some more.

But she didn't say another word.

After school I went right home. Beckie had told me to get back to school for six o'clock. The show kicked off at seven and she wanted me to be there in plenty of time. She hadn't told me what I needed to be there *for* but I wasn't going to argue with her. She was mad. I made it back to school for ten past six. Beckie was waiting for me by the gates.

"You're late!" she said. "Just get round to the back of the theatre and let Harj and Marcus sort you out."

I walked off before she hit me. All round the theatre were loads of kids dressed in weird outfits. Marcus was standing at the theatre doors.

"You here then, Number Two?" he asked with a grin.

"Very funny," I said. "How's yer mama?"

"Not half as cheap as yours," he answered. He was smiling like a madman.

"So what am I doin', then?" I needed to know.

Marcus stood to one side.

"In you go, Master Singh ... they're waiting for you," he said to me, his voice all posh.

"You what?" I asked.

"Just do it, Kully, before you shit yourself again," Marcus said.

I grinned this time.

"Like yer mum did?" I asked.

"Leave it!" he warned, but he was joking.

I walked past him and into the theatre. It was mad in there. There were people running around everywhere and the two drama teachers were running after them and shouting things like, "Do hurry along." Mrs Pincher was there too. She looked like she was about to have a heart attack.

"Oh, I do hope it runs smoothly!" she said about ten times to another teacher.

"I'm sure it'll all be fine," he was saying.

Marcus led me round the back of the stage.

"You bet it will," Marcus muttered.

Two Year Sevens walked past, both dressed as Harry Potter. "Where we going?" I asked.

"Just hurry up, blood. We ain't got time to arse about," Marcus hissed.

I saw Lexie standing with Ben and Mr Simms near the stage. The teacher had a list and he was checking the names of everyone going behind the stage. They had to go through the wooden doors.

"Just the stage hands back here!" he was shouting.

Marcus stopped and looked at me.

"Bollocks!" he said. "You gotta get back there, behind the stage. But you ain't gonna be on Simms' list ... he weren't there five minutes ago. I told you to hurry up."

"I'll go round the other side. Get backstage that way," I told him. There was another set of doors on the other side of the stage.

"No good," said Marcus. "Brimstone is that end. You couldn't get an ant on a diet past that freak."

"So what do we do?" I asked.

Just then I saw Ben grab another Year Seven Harry Potter. He grabbed his ear and pulled him away from the stage.

"OWWW!!!!" shouted the kid.

Simms looked over and started his "rudeboy" thing.

"Nah, blood ... what you doin', innit? Jus' allow dat pickney fe gwaan ..."

Even the Year Seven kid stopped moaning and looked at Simms like he was mental.

"He called my mum fat," said Ben.

"Just lef' it ... cool nuh," said Simms. I could see he didn't know if he should sort Ben and the Year Seven out, or carry on checking his list.

That was when Lexie moved in.

"Do you want me to take over for a moment?" she asked Mr Simms with a sweet smile.

"Oh, could you?" asked Mr Simms in his real voice.

"No problem," said Lexie. She took Mr Simms' list away from him.

"You're a real gem," Mr Simms said to her. The he turned back to Ben, who had the Year Seven kid by his other ear now. "Listen, rudebwoi," Mr Simms said. "Me done tell you to jus' allow dat pickney to pass tru ... seen?"

At that moment Marcus and I made for the door to get backstage.

We ran up the steps onto the stage, round the back of some thick black curtains. There were a few people around, testing things and moving stuff about. They ignored us. Marcus pointed towards some painted trees just on the right of the stage. They looked like they'd been painted by someone who'd never seen trees before. They looked more like brushes for cleaning the bogs with. Awful.

"You need to get behind them," Marcus said to me.

"And then what?" I asked.

"Then you wait," he told me. "Until Beckie's signal. And then you need to pull the rope that's behind you."

He walked me round to the back of the painted trees. No way was there enough space for me to hide back there. Just behind, a thick rope hung down from the roof.

"Just wait for the signal, then pull that and watch," Marcus said to me.

I was going to complain but I didn't. Instead I squeezed into the space behind the trees and waited.

Chapter 9

Yo!

I sat there for hours. I listened as everyone began to arrive and sit down. Mrs Pincher gave the most boring speech I'd ever heard. My feet went to sleep as ten Year Sevens, all dressed as Harry Potter, sang some sweet, sickly song. My arse went to sleep as a girl called Primrose Kaur Jones read out a long poem about how much she loved fluffy bunnies. In fact, by the time the pins and needles in my arms started, I was ready to cut off my ears and eat them with mustard. I'd sat there for over an hour and a half of the Christmas Special. Where the hell was my signal?

Ten minutes later I heard the 2.2 Massive come backstage. It was Mitesh that I heard first.

"We's gonna blow them away, you get me?" he was saying.

"Yeah, man," I heard Matt Peavey answer.

"Baddest crew in da world, blood," added Jitinder.

"Yeah, man," said Matt.

"Jus' let the 2.2 come on thru ..." bragged Mitesh. "Allow dat!"

"Yeah, man," said Matt Peavey for the third time. If I hadn't had pins and needles all over my body, I'd have jumped out from where I was hiding and punched him in the head. Just one more "yeah, man" was all it would have taken, but I didn't get the chance.

Then I heard something move behind me. I turned and peered round the stage. There were Lexie and Beckie. They were moving boxes around. Lexie saw me and winked.

The next person I heard was Mr Simms.

"Yes, blood," he said to someone. "Yuh ready?"

"You best believe it!" replied Jitinder.

"Two minutes, then," Simms told them.

I turned and peered round the trees onto the stage. The 2.2 Massive were ready for the show. They were all wearing the same outfits. They had bright yellow shell suits on with *2.2 Massive* written in red letters across the back. As well, they all had stupid baseball caps, all with the brims at different places on their heads. Mitesh was standing at the front, ready for the curtain to go up. The rest were behind him. They all had microphones. Over on the far side of the stage was their DJ. He had a jacket which said *DJ D-Struct* in big letters. He stood in front of a table with two record decks and a mixer on it.

I turned round and looked to see what Beckie and Lexie were doing. They both had what looked like garden hoses in their hands. They were pointing them towards the stage. Further along I saw Harj and Ben. They were doing the same. *What the hell did they need hoses for?* I thought to myself. That was when I heard bleating.

I spun round. Right in front of me was Mr Brimstone's enormous grey goat. Its eyes were like black marbles and its horns looked like they could cut through bone. And its breath stank worse than a monkey's armpit. I froze. What was I going to do? The goat looked mean and moody. If I got out from behind the cardboard trees, the 2.2 Massive

would see me. I knew I couldn't do that. I
didn't know what was going on, but I knew
I had to stay where I was.

I didn't move but I tried not to look at the
goat. Even so, every time I *did* look up it was
right there, looking hard at me.

Then I heard Mr Simms start the Grand
Finale. The 2.2 Massive were about to begin
their act. A beat came thumping through the
loudspeakers. It was so loud that it made the
goat jump.

The 2.2 Massive stepped forward onto the
main part of the stage.

"Now!" Beckie shouted.

No one heard her. The music was too
loud. Matt Peavey began his human beatbox
thing as Mitesh began to rap.

"Yo! Yo! 2.2 Massive comin' at ya! Don't
wanna catch ya! Yo! Yo!"

The rest of them were shouting "Yo!" too, copying Mitesh. They looked stupid.

I turned to Beckie. "When?" I shouted. She made that face – like someone was pulling out her stomach.

Water began to pour out of the hose she was holding. It began to pour out of everyone's hoses.

"Now!" she ordered.

I turned round and pulled on the rope. A sharp sound came from above me. It sounded like metal rubbing on more metal. Then I saw the long bits of metal from the builders' truck. The ones that Beckie's dad was going to fix the stage with. They were high above the stage. After I pulled on the rope the metal bits flipped over. Something began to fall onto the stage. DJ D-Struct saw it first. His mouth fell open. Loads of stuff that looked like mud began to hit the stage.

Beckie, Lexie and the others pointed their hoses at the piles of mud. Almost at once it turned into slush. But not just any old slush. As soon as the water hit the slush, a smell began to fill the theatre. A rich, strong, bitter smell. The smell of shit.

The water from the hoses spread the slush quickly.

One of the 2.2 Massive, Suresh, turned and slipped on it. He fell back on his arse, right into a big pool of the stuff. I looked out at the stage. The audience couldn't see us. As the 2.2 Massive Rap began to go badly wrong, the people watching weren't sure what the problem was. Then someone started to laugh. And then someone else. Soon half the audience were roaring with laughter.

That was when I saw Mitesh crawl towards where I was standing. His eyes were burning with anger. He tried to stand up but his feet slipped on the slush and he fell, face first. There was even more shit on him now. It was all over him. His cap had fallen off and there was stuff in his hair, all down his face, in his ears, and all over his clothes. He tried to get to where I was but Beckie saw him.

She pointed her hose towards Mitesh. Just in front of him was a big pile of dung. The water turned the dung to slime and splashed it up over Mitesh once more. The smell was terrible. Then I saw Mr Simms jump onto the stage. I grabbed the hose from Lexie. I knew he couldn't see me but I ducked down low anyway. Then I sprayed him. The look of shock in his face was amazing. He wobbled for a few seconds, trying not to fall over. Then he fell. He landed in the shit, face first.

"Come on!" I heard Ben shout. "We need to get out of here!"

"Let's go!" I told Lexie and Beckie.

The three of us turned and ran after Ben. We ran out of the back of the theatre and into the Beckie's dad's van. It was there waiting for us. Harj, Marcus and Ben were already in there, laughing their heads off. As I stepped into the back of the van, Beckie shouted, "Shut the doors!"

Just then I saw the goat. It was trotting out into the dark. It too was covered in shit from head to toe, but it didn't seem to care. It turned to me and I swear, it smiled. I began to wave at it – then I thought about what I was doing. I shook my head and shut the van door.

"Revenge!" Ben said to me, as I sat down.

"That was mad!" added Beckie.

"Madder than mad!" said Harj. "That's one of the funniest things I've ever seen."

The only person who wasn't laughing was me. I'd love to say that I was feeling bad about what we'd done, but I wasn't. I was worried about getting into trouble. Because

Mrs Pincher was going to go crazy. I told the others what I was thinking.

"Not a chance in hell," Beckie told us.

"Why's that?" I asked. "Someone must have seen us all round the back. And it was your dad who did the work, remember?"

"But someone broke into school last night," Beckie told us. "The police got called and everything. It was kids messing about. No one can blame my dad."

"What about us, then?" I asked her. "How do we get out of it?"

Beckie grinned.

"God – you're such a Number Two! We were all locked in this van. We missed the show. Someone played a prank on us."

Everyone else looked at each other as Beckie sat where she was and smiled sweetly.

I could hear people walking around outside the van. So could Beckie.

"Right everyone – just follow me and let me do the talking. OK?"

We all nodded. Beckie started to bang on the sides of the van. She was shouting "Help!" I looked at Lexie, leant over, gave her a kiss and then started to do the same. After about two minutes someone opened the door from the outside with the keys.

"Where did they get keys?" I asked Beckie, quickly.

"I left the keys in the door," Beckie told me. "If you hadn't been waving at that stupid goat, you'd have seen them."

The van door swung open. Mr Simms was standing in front of us. He stank. He was rubbing stuff out of his ears.

"What happened to you, sir?" asked Harj. He was trying hard not to smile.

87

"Never mind that, blood," said Mr Simms. "Why's you lot locked in a van?"

"Someone played a trick on us," Beckie lied.

"Who?" asked Mr Simms.

"Mitesh and Jitinder from the 2.2," I said.

"But they were just on stage," Mr Simms pointed out.

"We've been in here for hours," I moaned. "They locked us in before the show started."

"Really?" I could see Mr Simms wasn't sure.

I nodded. I made my face look all sad.

"You know how they call me Number Two?" I said to him.

Mr Simms went a bit red but nodded.

"Well they said that they were taking revenge. Of the Number Two, sir ..."

For a second Mr Simms looked grim. He looked around the van at all of our faces. Then he turned back to me.

"Did you say revenge *of* the Number Two?" he asked me.

I shook my head.

"No, sir. I said revenge *on* the Number Two," I told him.

He thought about that for a moment. Then he shook his head, told us to get out of the van and walked off. A stream of liquid poo made its way down the back of his neck. I turned to my friends and smiled.

"Thanks," I said to them all.

"Don't worry about it," Harj told me. "Besides, there's going to be a whole new load of Number Twos at this school now ... you're sorted."

I nodded.

"Fancy a snog?" I said to Lexie.

"Yeah!" she said.

I took her hand and walked off towards the school gates with her. Ben and Beckie were behind us. I heard them talking about who had thought up the plan. I didn't care. All I knew was that I was never going to get bullied again. Not for being a Number Two, anyway. And that felt great.

Barrington Stoke would like to thank all its readers for commenting on the manuscript before publication and in particular:

Susan Gillespie

Gareth Griffiths

Louise Richards

Jamie Trowsdale

Danny Wilson

Become a Consultant!

Would you like to give us feedback on our titles before they are published? Contact us at the email address below – we'd love to hear from you!

info@barringtonstoke.co.uk
www.barringtonstoke.co.uk

Two-Timer

Harj has no girlfriend and no hope. So when not one but two of the fittest girls in town ask him out, how can he say no? At first he feels bad about cheating on them ... then he starts to enjoy it. Soon lying becomes as easy as insulting his sister! But how long can he play this game?

Are You Kidding?

Marcus's grandad is the new school caretaker. That's embarrassing enough. But when the school mascot, Flossie the goat, goes missing, people start to ask tricky questions. Questions like, "Marcus, did your gramps eat our mascot?" Gramps is in big trouble. Can Marcus and his friends help him out?

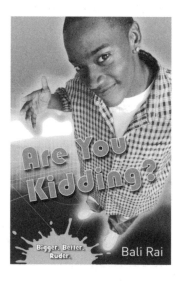

You can order these books directly from our website at
www.barringtonstoke.co.uk

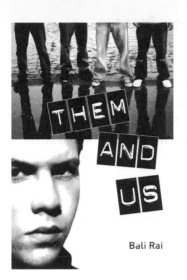